Tug-of-War

John Burningham

CANDLEWICK PRESS

For my mother, who introduced me to African folktales

First published in Great Britain in 2012 by Jonathan Cape,
an imprint of Random House Children's Publishers UK, A Random House Company

First U.S. edition 2013

Library of Congress Catalog Card Number 2012947722

ISBN 978-0-7636-6575-3

13 14 15 16 17 18 TLF 10 9 8 7 6 5 4 3 2 1

Printed in Dongguan, Guangdong, China

This book was typeset in Centaur MT.

Candlewick Press
99 Dover Street
Somerville, Massachusetts 02144

visit us at www.candlewick.com

Hare, Hippopotamus, and Elephant lived together in the forest.
Often, when Hippopotamus and Elephant had nothing
better to do, they would be mean to Hare and tease him.

Hippopotamus would say to Hare,
"What a tiny, wimpy thing you are,
with those ridiculous ears.
All you do is hop around."

And Elephant would say, "Hare, you really are a feeble idiot, with your twitching nose and whiskers. That's all you have."

Now, Hare was getting fed up with Hippopotamus
and Elephant being nasty to him day after day,
so he thought of a plan. Hare went first to see Elephant.

"Elephant," said Hare, "if we were to have a tug-of-war,
I think I would win."

"You must be joking, you sickly little twerp," said Elephant.
"I am two hundred million times stronger than you."

Nevertheless, Hare gave Elephant one end of a rope and
told him to wait for a tug and then to pull as hard as he could.

Hare took the other end of the rope and went down
to the river to talk to Hippopotamus.

"What on earth do you want now, you silly long-eared,
big-whiskered nerd?" said Hippopotamus.

"Although you think I am a tiny wimpy thing, if you have a tug-of-war with me," said Hare, "I know I would win."

"You! Win against me? You must be joking!" said Hippopotamus. "There is no way a little speck like you could possibly win against mighty me."

"Go on, then," said Hippopotamus, taking the other end of the rope. "When you start to pull, I'll tug so hard, you'll be flicked into the river."

Hare hid between Elephant and
Hippopotamus and tugged the rope.
In the river, Hippopotamus felt the tug
and started to pull.

In the forest, Elephant felt the pull on the rope
and was amazed at the strength of Hare.

And the tug-of-war began. Elephant
and Hippopotamus could not believe
how hard Hare was pulling the rope.

They pulled into twilight.
They pulled through sunset.

And they pulled all night long.

In the morning, Hare went as close as he could to Hippopotamus without being seen. "Oh, Hippopotamus, aren't you tired yet? You have been pulling

for such a long time. Won't you say I am as strong as you?"

"No, I won't, you weak little fool," said Hippopotamus,

and pulled even harder.

Hare hid near Elephant and asked, "Have you had enough, Elephant? Will you say I am the winner?"

"Not in a million years will you ever win against me," said Elephant, and pulled with all his might.

Hippopotamus pulled hard, but by now
he was getting very tired and could not
understand why Hare had not moved
and how he could be so strong.

"Have you had enough, Elephant?" Hare asked again.
"Do you admit that I am better than you?"

"Perhaps," said Elephant with a gasp,
"you are a little stronger than I had thought."

Then Hare tiptoed back to Hippopotamus.
"Oh, Hippopotamus," he said, "surely you
must now agree that I am the stronger one."

"You are not quite as weak as I had thought,"
Hippopotamus replied between tugs.

Some time later, Elephant and Hippopotamus pulled the rope close enough that they finally came face-to-face.

"What are you doing, Hippopotamus?" said Elephant. "I thought I was having a tug-of-war with Hare."

"So did I," said Hippopotamus.
Then they realized they had been tricked
and they were furious. "Let's get the little runt!"
they cried, and thundered off to find Hare.

"We'll search every inch of the forest
until we find that little weed,
and then we'll show him," they said.

But even though they charged around
for hours, they never found Hare,
because he was already miles away,
up in the hills.

For Hare had proved that although
he was not as strong as Elephant and
Hippopotamus, he was much more clever.